~Dedicated

To the people that matter to me most.

Who's There?

Chapter 1

Do you know what's lurking at the bottom of your garden? Have you ever seen it in the dead of night when all the adults are asleep? Have you ever looked out to see the stars when something catches your eye, moving beneath your dad's compost heap able to bear the stench of rotting veg. No? Well I have.

I had been allowed to stay up late one Friday night in the summer holidays after my sister's eighteenth birthday party. I was so tired I couldn't get to sleep and decided to do a bit of stargazing. Watching the distant planets through my telescope usually helped relax me, but it was pretty cloudy and I only caught a few glimpses of Orion's Belt or Whatever. By now you must be thinking I'm a bit of a nerd. Actually I am on the quiet. Not at school, then I'm just one of the lads who play soccer and mess with the girls new pencil cases, that sort of thing. I've always been good at science and I like it, the fact that you can make a circuit to get a robot into motion from your Meccano set, or use a microscope to see things a million times closer than normal really puts a smile on my face. Watching the stars burn light years away as though they are within my reach is my passion at the moment. Come on you'd have to be mad not to be into that sort of stuff. It's great to see how things work. Right? My mates would never understand. All they do is play soccer, watch soccer, play computer games and watch telly. The things we always do when we are all together. But this, the Universe, the Science, this is all mine... and that's when it happened. That night of my sister's birthday late in July, when the moon had finally risen and darkness descended upon our road. I was counting the stars I could see to try and push myself to sleep when something caught my eye at the bottom of the garden. At first I was sure I had imagined it and carried on counting. Then as I was feeling ready to drop off I saw it again. This time it didn't stop. On and on it went digging deeper into the ground. Deeper and deeper it went under the rotting carrots and cabbage, delving deep under the excess grass my dad had cut the week before. No matter how hard I tried I could not work out the shape of the strange object so at home in our garden. At first I thought it was probably a rat, but it was far too big. And besides there was nothing in the compost heap that would interest a carnivore, the visitor had to be an herbivore. See I told you I was a nerd! I opened my window to get a better look, the creature moved like lightning and was gone before I managed to stick my head out into the dark night air. So I waited. Late into the night when I heard all the usual signs that the adults were fast asleep, the crazy toilet flushes, my dad gargling like he's on Britain's got talent and my Mums 'tuneful' snoring. Then I knew it was safe to go outside and explore but was I going to be safe? I needed to be ready for anything.

Chapter 2

I got out of bed pulling on an extra jumper over my combat pyjama top and rooted around for my thick socks and boots. Next, protection! My water pistol – always ready for action and my trusty vicious catapult made by my Grandad (Mum was not pleased when he gave me the Y shapes branch with strong elastic and leather launcher and then showed me how to use it on her favourite plant pot!) It shoots things for miles, just right for tonight because I really don't want to be getting to close to that thing. Marbles! Perfect they could cause some damage launched in the catapult. Knee and elbow pads, I'm going to have to stay low, out of sight, who knows what could be out there? My night vision goggles and skateboard helmet. I was ready for it!

Creeping downstairs with all that gear on and a bag full of clanking glass balls is not the easiest thing I've had to do. Halfway down the stairs my Dad appeared for yet another trip to the loo! Seriously why don't adults do as they say? They always go on about me not drinking too much before bedtime; maybe they should take their own advice! Dad has at least 5 cups of tea before he finally goes to bed. Anyway, I know my Dad he will have been sleep, wee…I mean walking. So I carry on creeping down the stairs and head down the hall into the dark kitchen taking care not to nudge the stools at the counter. Mum always keeps the keys to the back door handy should there be an emergency. Why does everything sound so much louder when you need to be super quiet? Two turns of the latch – CLICK – and I am out!

Chapter 3

Standing there as still as I can be I realise how strange I must look. A kid pretending to be some stupid commando I'm so glad no one spotted me, especially my sister Hope. She would never let me forget it. So I turn to go back into the kitchen. That's when I know there is something out there! First I sense it. As though it is watching me, like I'm the odd one out there. Then I hear it! A low grunting noise, almost like a pig that has been swallowed whole by a whale. There is something strangely comforting about it, yet it is like no other noise I have ever heard and I seem think that it is trying to talk to me. Slowly I turn around peering in the dark totally forgetting about my night vision goggles, but I still can't see it, it is so well hidden somewhere around the compost heap, how it can stand the smell I've no idea especially on a warm summer night. I'm feeling a little brave and a lot stupid tonight so I crawl closer towards the veggie patch where Dads attempts at living off the land are fading and wilting. I take pity on the carrots, after all they are the only veg my Dad grows that I like so I whip out my water pistol and start giving the feathery leaves a good soak.

"Aaaaggggggggghhhhhhhhhhhhhhh!" The scream leaves my mouth before I have time to think about it. Suddenly the well hidden creature is hurtling towards me so fast, so scaly and so scarily, no longer hidden away, no longer a comforting noise, that low whale eating a pig noise has now become a very high squealing 'I'm going to eat you' noise, it gets louder and louder and closer and closer. I drop the water pistol and run. Run for my life! Reaching the back door in record time. The noise from the veggie patch has gone, I risk looking around, the creature has gone back to its hiding place as though nothing has happened. Shaking I open the kitchen door. Hearing footsteps on the stairs, I'm sure my scream must have woken the whole house up! What do I do? Stay out here with… It? Or face the music of whoever has come down the stairs. I suppose I could say I was sleep walking (I have been known to do that!) But wait, that won't work I'm all togged up for an adventure. There's only one thing for it. Silently I close the kitchen door and move out of sight. The light goes on I can see Mums bright blue dressing gown, then I hear water guzzling down the drain, then click- then click the light goes off... hang on a minute two clicks? Surely my own Mother hasn't just locked me outside in the dead of night with some scary beast roaming about the garden looking for a midnight snack. I can't believe she didn't check to see if anyone was out here, but then again why should she? All good little boys and girls should be safely tucked up in bed at this time of night!

Chapter 4

This is it then, the end of me Adam Fernlea aged 9 and three quarters! Well I'm not going without a fight. Plucking out my catapult I get ready to aim and load a marble into the launcher. This time turning on my night vision goggles (what a swizz! I still can't see a thing!) So blind to the night darkness with only my catapult to protect me I move to a better position so I can see the whole garden. I sit tight up against the wall behind a large plant pot and the watering can to wait. I wait, and I wait, and I close my eyes – No! Got to stay awake. I wish I had my water pistol I could at least use the water to wake me up a bit. I really don't fancy dipping my hand into the watering can water, I'd probably end up catching a frog or something tonight. So I wait, and I wait and I wake up with the sun shining on my face, my water pistol in my hand, an upturned watering can and a very cross mum looking down on me!

"What on earth have you been doing out here all night? Wait until your father hears about this, what will the neighbours think? Quick you little urchin, get inside before Mrs Devlin from number 17 sees you. She will call the Police on us if she thinks I've let you stay out all night like you're on some kind of SAS Mission! Inside! NOW!"

No time to explain, not that I could anyway, surely it wasn't all just a dream. I'm not that imaginative… am I? But how did I get my water pistol back? Must have been a dream right? The only explanation! Funny though I still felt as though I was being watched when mum was yelling at me. What do you think?

Chapter 5

Mum kept an especially close eye on me all that day. I couldn't even look out of the window without being told to stop daydreaming and go and do my homework. At least my teacher is pleased with me this morning. I'm the first person to finish all my homework and she says it's a miracle and hopes I will continue to be as enthusiastic with our next topic, "Embroidery through the years". Embroidery, come on! What does she think I am? I have bigger things to think about than sewing nice little pictures onto colourful pieces of cloth. Even the girls are moaning about it so you know it must be bad. Why can't we learn about something exciting, like the planets or the Egyptians or dinosaurs – how cool would school be then? One thing is for sure, I would definitely not keep getting told off for daydreaming!

After an hour of our teacher going on about something called running stitch, back stitch, French knots and chain stitch I really was all set for a daydream, when the bell rang for break-time. At last, time to think about what had actually happened on Saturday night and what my next step should be. How was I ever going to get out of the house again at night to investigate? Who could I trust not to laugh me out of the school gates and make my life hell? Well one thing is for sure that is Simon Bagshaw out! He's much too much of a know it all, he would think I was in cloud cuckoo land. Come to think of it so would I if someone had told me there was some weird creature attacking them in the middle of the night for a water pistol I would think they had totally lost the plot. I need someone who is quiet, clever and well got nothing to lose by believing my story! Right that'll be the new lad Davey Green then! I know exactly where to find him! As usual there he is sat under the big tree behind the girls practicing their dance routines. He's alone, playing marbles, while all the other lads are charging about, or yep you guessed it playing football!

"Hi, fancy a game?" I ask as Davey looks up in surprise, I think he has forgotten what it's like to be spoken to by another lad. He is quiet for so long I nearly turn around and go back to kicking a hole in the dirt next to the make shift footie pitch.

"Ok!" He finally replies. So I sit and we knock a few marbles backwards and forwards. I know break will be coming to an end soon so I just go ahead and blurt it all out…

"I know how this sounds" I begin in a rush "but well there is something, some animal at the end of our garden and it charged at me the other night, boy was I scared but I'm sure it told me it was thirsty and really needed the water from my water pistol because my Dad's compost heap was too dry, but I was too scared by the noise it made and with the speed it moved that I screamed like a girl, dropped the water pistol and headed inside. My mum was just coming down the stairs though I knew she would have a fit so I had to go back outside. She locked me out! My own mum! She didn't know I was there but even so, I had to stay outside with that thing there, grunting and squealing around the garden, all night! When I woke up though I had my water pistol with me, hang on a mo, the watering can, it was empty Davey, can you believe it? I was right! It did talk to me, it was thirsty, I'm not going mad! I've got to find out what it is, it's amazing. I need to get out of the house! How am I going to do that? Mum found me outside and went crazy so I'm grounded forever!" Then the bell went! Davey started to pack away his marbles, he couldn't even look at me, he must have thought I'd lost all of mine!

"See you in class" he muttered, and slowly, carefully he picked his way over jumpers and cardigans left all over the grass. He was first in line ready to get back into class, back to work – even if it was embroidery! Sensible old Davey, what was I thinking telling him like that?

Chapter 6

It was just after tea when the phone rang. It is always for Hope, so I left the table, along with my peas and mash hoping Mum wouldn't notice and decided to go try out the new game I had bought out of my pocket money. I was half way up the stairs when I heard my mum say my name, in that way that could only mean trouble!

"Adam, yes, why? What on Earth has he been up to now?" I knew something was going on so I had to stay and listen. So I crouched down at the top of the stairs, trying to find out exactly what the conversation was all about. I was expecting it to be long and painful but suddenly my mum said "No problem, that's fine, I'm sure he won't mind, Goodbye! Adam, you can stop lurking about at the top of the stairs and if you come down right now I shall tell you all about the conversation I have just had without you having to eavesdrop!" How do mums do that? Always know where you are and exactly what you're doing sometimes even before you do?

Dragging my feet I thump down the stairs. I've no idea what I've done this time, I mean apart from camping out on the patio all night at the weekend I didn't think anything else could be quite as bad as that.

"That was Davey's Mum! What have you been saying to him at school?" I couldn't believe it! What a horror, I didn't think he would go and tell his mum on me, I suppose I can just say it was a story to try and frighten him or something.

"Davey's mum is quite excited, it seems you are the first person that has actually tried to make friends with him since he moved here last term and Davey's mum is very eager for him to try to make new friends and well, fit in a bit better. She says he can be a bit shy and that some boys have been quite mean to him because he is quite clever and enjoys school. Anyway, given your behaviour this weekend I really shouldn't even be asking you this but Davey's mother was very insistent, so would you like to have a sleep over at Davey's house on Friday?" I'm astounded! He actually believed me! He didn't think that I was a total fruit cake! "So?" said my mum "would you like to go? I mean I've never really heard you mention him before, but if he is a nice boy then I am all for it, what do you think? Shall I let her know that you will go there straight after school on Friday?" Nodding my head I try to keep the enormous grin from spreading all over my face, my stomach was doing somersaults, someone actually believed me! Not only that, but that someone was the cleverest lad in the school and he had a plan. He must have a plan, or at least an idea otherwise why would he want to meet up out of school?

Chapter 7

I can't wait until Friday, every day seems to drag and I haven't even managed to talk to Davey about his plan, there always seems to be something or someone in the way. Finally on Thursday Afternoon Davey tells our teacher that he needs my help with some computer work. Mrs Graham nearly falls off her chair before nodding her head and saying, "Ok Davey, that's fine if you need him. Adam is that ok with you?" Simon makes daft noises and starts sniggering at the back of the class.

"Yyy-yes, that's fine" I say unsure as to what we are supposed to be doing on the computer. Maybe I will actually get a good mark in ICT if I pair up with Davey I'm sure he knows what we should be doing. We walk towards the corridor when we hear Mrs Graham booming, " I don't know what you think is so funny Simon Bagshaw. If you don't get that piece of embroidery finished there will be no computers at all for you!" Davey grins, I think it's the first time I've ever seen him smile.

"Should be nice and quiet in the computer room this afternoon if they've got to finish all that sewing."

"Yeah ta so much for getting me out of that one, at least if I have to take it home my Gran can help me untangle the mess I've gotten into... So, you believed me the other day then? You didn't think I was a bit funny in the head?"

"Well, you have to admit it is a bit far fetched, but you must think that you saw something otherwise you wouldn't have blurted it all out to me, and anyway I'm always looking for a new project. Chances are it was a Muntjac or some other small deer that you startled! Have you got anything you want to research for this lesson then?" He asked as he logged onto the computer, "I do most of mine at home so I'm not bothered what we look at." I think for a minute, so many things go through my head.

"I dunno! I'd like to know more about space and the planets and stuff, maybe even learn more about the dinosaurs they were pretty cool! I don't know much about the Egyptians, or the Romans come to think of it, maybe I should be doing more research at home too!" There's silence as Davey clacks away at the keyboard with amazing speed.

"Right, Our Universe it is then, that way I can talk my mum into letting us spend the night in the tree house stargazing."

"Oh?" I can't seem to keep the surprise out of my voice, "I mean, aren't we a bit old for tree houses and stuff?"

"You haven't seen my tree house. It has actually got a fantastic telescope and you will get a good view of Venus if it is a clear night on Friday but I also have lots of other gear up there. You know, like for surveillance and stuff. My Dad used to work for this technology company and I got all his prototypes that he didn't need anymore or didn't quite do the job properly." Davey began pulling bits of electrical kit out of his school bag. "All you need to do is set up these mini cameras in your garden near to where you saw the creature, it's really easy to do! Then we can watch it from up in the tree house, if that sounds ok?" I ruffle Davey's over long hair, "you

did have a plan after all didn't you!"

Chapter 8

It was quite easy to set up the cameras that Davey gave to me. Thinking about how the creature seemed to want water I placed a tub underneath one of the cameras, it was worth a try! Then I go inside to think about what to pack. I need all the usual stuff I don't want my mum getting suspicious. Tracksuit, sleeping bag, my most recent comic, secret chocolate supply that I have always managed to hide from Hope. She's a maniac when she has a row with her boyfriend and always comes snooping around my room for goodies. She has no idea I managed to loosen the floorboard in my cupboard, the space was perfect for the old fashioned money box my Granddad gave me. It holds so much more valuable stuff than money now though; it's almost like a time capsule of my whole life. Underneath all the usual stuff I bury my torch and catapult I know mum will want a quick look to make sure I have everything I need, oops nearly forgot best put in a clean pair of socks and undies or she will pull everything back out of the rucksack and repack it.

Mum goes on and on about making a good impression on Davey's mum all through breakfast, and how nice it would be for me to have a nice normal, reliable friend I could bring home and do homework with! Does she really think that is the normal behaviour of a (nearly) 10 year old boy? I do manage to pack a few more goodies into my rucksack while she is going on though. Then she gives me the longest hug and the most embarrassingly smoochy kiss ever, and I'm on my way! I have no idea how I am going to get through the day. I am so excited about what we will see on the monitor, I mean what could it be? Just one of those jack deer things, what was it again? A Muncjac that was what he called it. It looked too small though and it would have to have been an enormous rat, maybe a hare, or a badger although I'm not sure there are any round here. A fox, that's it, it must have been a small fox, a baby. I've never heard them make a noise like that but I suppose he must have been as scared as I was. I'm not sure about the asking for water thing either, must have just been imagining that one. Still, even getting to see a fox close up like that will be very cool. I might even be able to use the computer to show it to the class, Miss'll love that!

Chapter 9

We have the world's most boring Assembly today about road safety. I know it is important especially for the little kids, but how many times did we need to see a flashing light and reflector? "Be Safe- Be Seen!" Wear a reflector on your coat, on your bag, on your snooze, I mean your shoes. Have a light on your bike, on your scooter, on your arm. Wear a bright yellow visibility jacket on your way to and from school, on your bike, on your scooter. Do they really think us kids don't do all this stuff anyway? My mum won't let me out of the house unless I'm fully padded, brightly clothed and lit up like a Christmas tree. The little ones did seem to like the teddy bear reflectors they were given though so I suppose it was worth the 40 minutes of total boredom suffered by everyone else. Even Mrs Graham kept glancing at her watch every five minutes, and poor old Mr Potts had to be nudged awake more than once! Finally after the longest day in history the end of the day bell rang!

I looked over at Davey as he put a bag bigger than my overnight bag onto his back. Yep definitely picked the right guy to help me out! I can't wait to see this 'Techno Tree-house!' I mean how cool would it be to have all that stuff, hidden away from Hope but to be able to spy on her and her weird friends. I could get her into some serious trouble with mum! She would never be allowed to baby sit me ever again!

Chapter 10

'Wow' I am not disappointed; Davey's tree-house looks more like a tree village. It's huge, made of proper wood with windows and what looks like a huge bubble stuck to the side of the tree that overlooks the fields at the back of his house. A spiral staircase has been attached to the tree leading to a trap door underneath the floorboards of the house. Davey unlocks the combination lock and we pull ourselves up inside the tree-house. The trunk of the tree goes straight through the middle and has a couple of hammocks hanging from it. Davey puts his bag in one, I do the same with the other. Suddenly a loud buzzing noise wails all around us making me jump. "Just my mum!" Davey explains as he goes over to the telephone on the wall. "Yes mum, we're here, no we don't need anything. Ok I'll ask... Mum wants to know if you need anything?" Davey says with eyes looking upwards. "I'm ok thank you Mrs Green" I shout. Davey listens again "No mum, he's ok. I know but... ok... yes that's fine mum! Ok...alright, I'll ask him..." This time Davey covers the mouthpiece. "Sorry, Mum wants to know if pizza from the take away down the road is ok? What kind you prefer or whether you would like her to make you something?" he says with embarrassment! "Pizza's great, any kind" I say smirking, it seems to me that all mums are the same, they don't mean to be embarrassing but well they always manage to be just that! Davey's conversation continues with his mum..."Ok, thanks mum" he says as he hangs up "she'll buzz us when arrives." I can't believe it, "And that's it?" I stutter with amazement. "No, 'but you need some vegetables with that', or, 'what about your homework,' or, 'have you washed your hands?'" Davey shakes his head and gives me a puzzled look. Humph, maybe all mums aren't the same after all!

Chapter 11

The bubble on the side of the tree-house turns out to be an enormous telescope, making mine look like a cheap toy. I'm glad I didn't bring it. Davey sees me looking at the massive piece of kit with awe. "My Dad knew a man, who knew a man that no longer wanted it. It was just before he moved out so I think it was a bit of a guilt present. It is great though. You'll get a good view tonight it being so clear. If you keep checking you could write up a night sky diary to go with your computer work and I'll print out the charts to show you know what you're talking about. You'll get the best grades you've ever had!" I can't believe I've never really got to know Davey before, he's actually really cool as well as being really clever and the stuff he's got hidden away up here is amazing. I recognise some of the stuff like real night vision goggles and the most up to date laptop I've ever seen which he click, clicks away at while three more monitors show various views from around the tree-house, these must be the surveillance screens where I will see pictures from the cameras I planted in the garden. One flickers and fuzzes out before I see a very familiar veggie patch appearing before me. "Cool, that's my dad it is so clear!" I watch as he potters about between the compost bin the plants and the sheds. "I sure hope the creature stays well hidden until my dad goes inside, I don't know who would be more freaked out, it or my dad!" Davey and I crease up with laughter at the thought until the buzzer interrupts us. "Pizza" Davey shouts as he lifts up the trap door and the delicious smell makes us realise how hungry we both are.

Chapter 12

Davey and I chomp our way through some of the pizza, putting the rest in his fridge for breakfast! I think I've gone to kid heaven!!! It will be a few hours before it is fully dark so with Davey click clicking away I try out the hammock. Turns out it is surprisingly comfortable. I must have dropped off because it is pitch black when I wake up wondering where on Earth I am, and why I am rocking gently backwards and forwards. The only light in the room is an eerie green glow coming from the bank of surveillance monitors in front of Davey. Finding my torch I tiptoe over to the extra seat, I'm not sure if Davey is asleep with his eyes open as he looks totally mesmerised by the grainy dark images shifting in front of him. "Seen anything yet?" I ask, but there is no answer. I look more closely at him. He's as white as a sheet, well actually he's green but I'm not sure if it's just the light from the monitors. His mouth is hanging open, dribble forming on his lower lip, ready to drop. He could have been sat here for hours it's really not a good look, he must be asleep. So like you see in all the good movies I wave my hand frantically up and down in front of his face. Finally he turns his astonished face towards me and points at the monitor, it all just looks like a fuzzy picture of our garden to me. That is until I notice something moving at the bottom of the screen, then suddenly it's in the middle of the screen, then back to the bottom again. Whatever it is seems to be collecting something. The longer I look the more clearer things become, soon I've got my bearings. It's collecting the pea pods and storing them at the back of the compost heap, racing at such a speed I can only just make out the blur as it moves about on screen. It seems to be about the size of a small dog but only running on its hind legs, like a bird, kind of. I know it is too small to be an ostrich or emu and anyway there are no ostrich farms or zoos near here for one to have escaped from, and I can't make out any feathers. It's quite skinny but fast, boy can that thing run! No wonder I had no time to think the other night. The creature stops abruptly and pokes it's head up as though it senses us watching it. Secretly I hope my sister Hope has suddenly decided to go on a midnight tour of our garden, but no, it comes closer to the camera, the one near to where I placed the bowl of water. Davey finally springs into action, out of the corner of my eye I see him taking a still image of the creature changing and enhancing it on another screen, but I can't take my eyes of the live pictures as it comes closer and closer, so close now I can see its scaly head, its eyes seem to pierce right through the camera lens over the gardens and into Davey's tree house, staring at me, straight into my eyes. "Thank you" the voice in my head is easier to understand than other night. "Thank you" it says again as the creature reaches down and begins to lick at the water beneath the camera. Davey's fantastic technology has made the picture so clear, it could be standing right there in front of us in the daylight. Another few clicks and he has started an image search on the internet. I flick my eyes back to the screen but the creature has vanished. Davey is staring at me agog for the second time in the last ten minutes, finally he manages in a squeaky sort of voice, "Dinosaur". "Yeah? I thought more like a baby ostrich or something escaped from the zoo" I said hopefully! Davey shook his head. "Dinosaur." He muttered again as he grabbed my chin over to his screen to look at the image he had found from his search. Not exactly sure what to take in I look at the pictures. I have to admit that yes they do look a lot like the living thing I've just seen (and heard although I'm keeping that to myself for a bit) on the screen in front of me but, really? I know I'm nowhere near Davey when it comes to knowing what's new in the world, but I am pretty sure that there have been no 'dino' births in at least, oh, the last 64 million years! It could just be a really big prank that someone is playing on us, there is that kids prank show on the telly after all! I wouldn't put it past our Hope if she thought it would get her on the telly, and ridicule me at the same time!

Davey's mouth has finally begun to work, and although he is babbling a bit it seems he is sure the creature is a relative of the dinosaur known as the 'Lesothosaurus'. A herbivore, thankfully, around in the Jurassic era found in what we now know as South Africa. It seems it made a burrow down in the Earth where it was cooler. "Maybe" Davey is saying, "maybe an egg has laid deep in its burrow under your dad's compost heap for the past 64 million or so years and has finally incubated due to the heat and chemicals created by the rotting vegetation." My turn to stare in amazement! The kid has lost it, gone completely bonkers does he not realise it is just a hoax? "Listen" I say trying to get him to see sense. "This is probably just my sister's idea of an early Halloween joke. I admit she has gone too far this time and she's gone to a lot of trouble with the robotics and whole creation, it looked quite realistic but really Davey think about it! A dinosaur! In my back garden! Get real! And anyway surely up here in the middle of England we're an awfully long way away from South Africa. It's not like a dinosaur could have caught Jurassic Airways to come here for his Jollies, there must have been oceans and stuff, different bits of land to get over not to mention the mighty T-Rex. It's just a story, a good one but a tale all the same. You'll see, on Monday we will be the laughing stock of the school!" Davey sighed, "I know it seems as though it could never happen Adam. But it has. I mean anything is possible! We don't really know anything about dinosaurs yet, only bits and pieces that we've put together from all over the world. They keep finding loads out. Only last year they discovered some dinosaurs actually island hopped either by swimming over seas or migrating and then being cut off by the rising tides, so really anything is possible! And they think that the Maisaura used to lay their eggs in a ditch and cover it with vegetation which would keep the eggs warm and it would incubate them whilst they kept watch and gathered food. Imagine it

Adam! Imagine if it has happened once, it could happen again! We might well be able to bring the dinosaurs back Adam! Imagine having a Stegosaurus or a triceratops as a pet...I have to see it, your dinosaur I mean, the one in your garden. I have to see it tonight with my own eyes! I'll get my tent, we can camp, in the garden!" "Yeah, great" I mutter not sure I'm ready for a face to face confrontation with anything more prehistoric than my Gran's slippers!

Chapter 13

By the time Davey has packed every thing he thinks he will need we might as well have just packed up the entire tree-house! Davey's mum was so pleased he had a friend that she didn't even check up when I said I had texted my mum and it was ok for Davey to stay the night. I didn't mention that my sister was to be in charge as my Mum and Dad were going to their monthly ballroom dancing event at my Aunts and they don't usually get back until after Sunday lunchtime. I also didn't mention that Hope gets so involved in her music and face-timing that she wouldn't know if we were in the house or not! That is my plan though to get her back. As soon as I can convince Davey that this whole thing is just a joke, we will think of a plan to rival Hope's. She may have clever mates in electronics and be good with a sewing machine but I've got my secret weapon! Davey! With all of his technology we will have Hope screaming like a little girl!

Davey's tent takes five minutes to pop up but it takes most of the day to organise power, signals and lighting so that all of his high-tech gear will be of use. Hope just stands around watching with a sly smile on her face. Dad is none too happy with the cameras in his veggie patch! I can't believe he thinks we have been spying on him, does he think we kids have nothing better to do? Thinking about it, how do we explain those cameras? "Well, you see Mr Fernea, Adam and I have a very interesting project on the go, it's called 'garden creatures, friend or foe'. Adam happened to mention you had had a problem with Aphids on your pea pods, so we thought we would get some micro footage. I plan to unleash my secret weapon, if it is ok with you Mr Fernlea?" "Well now then Davey I'm not sure I want anyone experimenting with my vegetables...." Begins my dad, until Davey butts in! You've got to hand it to the kid, he thinks on his feet, and he's got all the answers with grown ups! I can't believe he's managed to shut my dad up before he gets started on organic growing and how pesticides are bad for us as well as the Earth. "Don't worry Mr Fernlea, I'm only talking about the colony, well a loveliness of Ladybirds to give it its official term, I've been breeding some especially to see how they deal with those dreadful little garden pests, but my Mum doesn't have any veggies to test out my theories on, so is that ok with you if I use your wonderful specimens?" My dad is speechless! That is something I've never managed to achieve! Davey certainly knows how to make things go his own way. My dad mumbles something about it being fine and he must go as he can hear my mum calling him, although I know from the water running down the drain that she is actually in the shower! Hope too has disappeared, I'm sure she is up to something. Maybe we should set up surveillance in her room.

Chapter 14

Mum and Dad left and will now be fox-trotting their way around some village hall somewhere. Strictly Come Dancing has a lot to answer for! I really shouldn't have to see my parents parading about in front of my friends wearing sequins and Cuban heels! I shouldn't even know about Cuban heels! Anyway Hope has disappeared into her lair so I know now is the time to talk to Davey. "So I'm thinking we should put some kind of listening device in Hope's bedroom, that way we can work out how to get our own back." "Own back on who?" "Oh sorry, I didn't realise you had your headphones on, I was just saying Hope, I'm sure this is something to do with her probably some textile animatronics project for college and she decided to have a laugh!" Davey looks confused, "Do you really think she has nothing better to do than try and scare you out of your wits? And anyway there is no way my electronics are wrong on this!" He holds you a test tube with seriously bad smelling contents; I gag as he wafts it under my nose. "What is that?" I ask already knowing the answer. "Poo! Dinosaur poo to be exact Adam and not the coprolites you find in a museum. This is genuine fresh as you like Dinosaur poo! So no I don't think putting a microphone in your sister's room would help do you?"

To be honest I'm not sure if it was the smell or the thought of what Davey had just told me but I had to sit down, quickly! Davey doesn't seem to notice. In fact he is so busy twiddling knobs and turning switches I think he has forgotten I am there he is in total geek mode. He jumps as I begin to speak "No! I'm sure it is just more of my sister's elaborate plan to get me really worried, then she won't have to look after me anymore because Mum and Dad won't feel they can leave me with her if I'm seeing things. There is no way this is real Davey. Look lets pack up all these gadgets and just camp out, old fashioned style, midnight feasts, ghost stories to tell. NO ELECTRONICS NO DINO TALK OK?" Davey pulls a plug and suddenly the electronic whirring that I hadn't previously noticed stopped and there was just the sound of my sisters out of tune singing and the beat of her latest favourite tune.

Chapter 15

I should have known not to trust Davey. There was no way he would give up just like that. It had taken him hours to set up cameras, heat seeking sensors, microphones, and a whole load of other equipment I never knew existed let alone thought someone of our age would be able to use. But then again Davey is not your typical 10 year old, the kid is a technological genius! It's dark in the tent when the scuffling noise outside woke me up. Dark that is except for the black and white image flickering on the small screen beside Davey's head. I creep over and have a look. There was the same small shape I had seen before, nosing about outside the tent. Then I hear the voice in my head. "It's ok, I mean no harm I wanted to say thank you for the water and ask if maybe you could help me?" Scared is not the word! Surely that's all in my head! Must be a lack of sleep or too much cheese before bedtime? After all it is only a cat out there, right?

I think about waking Davey but I was almost positive it was just a cat, it had to be! So I pick up Davey's night vision goggles and slowly open up the zip of the tent. The scuffling stops, there you go I'm thinking definitely a cat, I've scared it away. I re-zip the opening of the tent and sink back onto my camping gear. "I'm still here" the voice in my head said, "promise I don't bite!"

Chapter 16

There is suddenly something scary, cold and eerie about being camped outside in our back garden with no adults about to shout to in an emergency. Just me, my 'I don't care what you do' sister and some technologically advanced nerd of a friend who I couldn't help but blame for the situation. The technologically advanced nerd who is currently sleeping in peace as though everything in the world was fine and his best mate wasn't going to be devoured by some weird alien creature from an as yet undiscovered planet. It could talk to me though some kind of ESP for goodness sake it could be frying my brain as Davey sleeps! I kick his foot sharply but he just murmurs something about not wanting to go to football. "Let him sleep," the voice in my head is back, "I really need you to trust me, I trust you. I am in danger but you are safe and you are the only one who can help me! Please come out and meet me face to face. I need protection I am alien to your new world, my species is from many, many years ago. It is by some strange changes to the Earth here where my burrow is that I seem to have incubated into life. I have spent my childhood in darkness eating the rotting tree roots and such buried deep within the soil but now along with a great thirst for water, I have become more curious as to this world above. The world I can hear from far beneath but have only ever glimpsed through moonlight and dawn. My eyes grow more accustomed to the light but I am safer in the darkness. If I was to be discovered in your world I could not imagine what would become of me. Please understand this message and meet me."

Chapter 17

I have no option. I have to meet this thing head on. I am sure with what Davey has already told me that I am facing some kind of prehistoric creature which has somehow miraculously come to life. Although I can't help thinking that this is actually all a dream, I mean what are the odds of this creature being awoken by some strange fluke in my back garden underneath my dad's compost heap and then actually being able to communicate with me. It sound like... well it sounds like something out of some story book! This thing, outside, I mean is it possible it can be friendly or is it just lulling me, trying to get me out for some sinister reason? Surely if it is from another time it is going to be dangerous, it might even be a meat eater...oh no wait it could have devoured me the first night I saw it, then gone on a mad rampage throughout the village but it didn't. It just scurried back to its hiding place. Suddenly now that I am thinking rationally (well as rationally as someone can, who thinks they can speak with dinosaurs) I am curious, how long has the creature been hiding out and why here, why now, why is it able to get into my head? I'm a ten (yes yes, almost 10!) year old boy! What would you do?

You guessed it, I had no option really, I just had to find out what was going on. Before I could over think it any further I pull up the zipper of the tent and stuck my head bravely out into the fresh, dark night air.

Slowly, looking around, I wrench my feet from my sleeping bag and emerge from the tent, PJ's and stocking feet. Not really the best attire to meet a new species but if I go back into that tent I'm not sure I will have the courage to re-emerge ever again. I hear the now familiar snuffling noise coming from the cabbage patch it stops as I begin walking towards it. "Um, Hi…" I try out loud, "are you still there?" "Oh I'm here Adam, and I'm as real as you and your friend sleeping in that woven orb. I thought the great square stone burrows that house so many were odd enough but what protection does that give you? Even I am aware of the wetness that flows freely from above and how it drenches everything in its path. Sadly though it has not flowed down to my burrow for many moons, which is why I was forced up from the trees life systems where did the… what do you

48

call it?" "Water" I think to myself. "Ahh, yes, where did the water go to?" I can't stop myself I seem to answer the questions automatically in my head and the creature knows the answers almost before I do. It's time for me to get some answers now. "What are you anyway? How come you know so much about me and what do you want from me?" I think for starters. "Help, I need help Adam. I need to stay undiscovered, I am sure in this new world if a living prehistoric creature was found there would be many questions and your species would be worried of a resurgence of mine, especially the forceful ones which feasted upon the weaker. I only know what you know Adam, I know I am from another time, and that your friend thinks I am a dinosaur, a terrible lizard. I am not Adam! I will cause you no harm. Your kindness has linked us in this way making communication possible. All I can tell you about myself is that I seem to have been born from an egg which lay deep beneath the surface, something happened, and the egg, me... hatched. I managed to grow and survive eating and drinking my surroundings. When I was big enough I began to dig. First I started but the heat seemed to burn though my skin. I knew no life could sustain the heat so I began to dig up, and up, there was more food, and it was a good deal more habitable but then my burrow grew dry and I had to dig again. Suddenly out I came into the brightness. I was stunned and fell backwards into the hole I had dug. When I came around it was dark, and cool, and I could forage."

Well I did ask! I suppose it makes sense in a kind of science fiction way. What are the odds of this happening? My dad's smelly old compost heap starting a chain reaction to resurrect the dinosaurs! Could happen... I suppose!

Chapter 18

"Ok, I think I need to wake Davey, find out for sure what you are but I agree, whatever we find out you must be kept a secr..."

"ADAM! ADAM! GET AWAY, MOVE NOW" Great, now my sister decides that she cares enough about me to save me from some unknown creature. As I stand there dampness soaking into my stocking feet I realise Hope is holding out her mobile phone yelling incoherently into it, but I get the idea, she thinks it is some kind of animal escaped from the zoo. I look at the creature and we both know what to do.

Quickly I duck in the tent and viciously shake Davey awake! Seriously how can the kid sleep with my screechy sister yelling the neighbourhood down? I hiss at him "Davey, emergency, no questions, it is NOT dangerous. Take the creature! Hide it! GO!! Leave everything just GO!" And just like that of he goes, no ifs, no buts, just him and the weird new species we had just discovered following close behind.

Hope is still screaming something about the creature carrying Davey off in its teeth. My sister is amazing! Even though she has just witnessed Davey running off with the creature she has convinced herself that some wolf or a lion has escaped and taken my best friend off to become its midnight snack! She is so hysterical that snatching the phone from her is easy. Fortunately Hope has only called mum and dad and well they are used to her overreacting. Mum is fine once I tell her it was just one of Davey's realistic remote control robotic animals for our science project. She makes me promise to sleep indoors tonight though and make sure Hope is ok. I must admit she does look a little shell shocked when I hand her back the phone. Mind you it must have looked very odd to see your little brother talking to a real live dinosaur. I suppose I can forgive her for freaking out a little. I struggle to keep my giggles in as I lead her back inside. Mum said something about getting Hope a herbal tea or something but I think she might be better going up to bed.

As I come down to make sure the tent and gear is all secure. I notice a car light outside the front. I open the door ready to tell mum they should have stayed, and that Hope is already fast asleep, but it's not

their car. It's a car I don't recognise.

Chapter 19

Ok that's not good! Looks like someone was either spying or listening in. No matter! There's no proof we found....Oh no! Yes there is, Davey's camera was still running the whole time. It's still in the tent and I didn't even get to lock it. I creep towards the kitchen window where flashlights sweep the garden. They spot the tent and are in quick as lightening, the two men bring out Davey's equipment and start examining it. I have no choice I need to get to Davey's. We need to help the creature together.

Grabbing the first pair of shoes I can I carefully leave the house via the front door then leg it all the way to Davey's Techno tree-house.

I can see the lights flickering as I get closer to his hideaway. Surely the creature isn't up there as well! I knock on the hatch and Davey eyes wide and gleaming starts with his findings. "He's a dinosaur alright Adam, I can't believe it, what was your dad chucking onto his compost heap. It had some thermo-radioactive reaction and permeated through the soil to the Lesothosaurus egg buried way beneath the Earth's surface." "Davey, its half past midnight, I've just had to lie to my mum, put my hysterical sister to bed, and run from two guys who seem to have been spying on us for some reason, please just tell me what's going on?" "I just did! Don't you see? Your dad managed to warm up the earths soil and send down all the right nutrients to make the dormant egg incubate and somehow your Lesothosaurus, that's what we call this kind of dinosaur anyway, managed to live and now I'm guessing it needs our help. Two guys you said. Did they take the camera? What kind of car was it?" "Yeah the camera and the rest, listen we need a plan. We have to make a life like animatronic Lesothosaurus creature otherwise my family are going to get suspicious. Um where's the creature gone?" "Davey, Davey, is that you? Did you and Adam have a fight? There's someone here to see you love, says it is important. Something about an escaped animal from the zoo I'd feel better if you slept inside tonight. Oh hello Adam, did you decide to stay here after all? You had better come in too." Mrs Green constantly looks about nervously as if some great beast will leap and attack at any moment. "Oh, yes sorry Mrs Green we just got a bit caught up in the animatronics homework. Davey has created such a life like creature, we took it over to scare Hope earlier and I'm afraid she went a little bit crazy. There is no wild animal on the loose, just a joke that went too far. Sorry."

We follow Davey's mum into the kitchen, I instantly recognise the two men from my garden. Plus they have all of Davey's equipment in their hands. They smile politely at Mrs Green as she relays my story. Davey can't seem to keep still and shuffles his feet nervously, it's only when I look down I realise I have on one of my own black trainers and a pink leopard print trainer on the other foot. "Did you leave in a hurry son, or is that the new fashion?" the smallest of the men asks. "Well sir, my sister was not very happy when she found out we played a trick on her so yes I suppose I did leave in a hurry." "You managed to pick up the creature though, must be heavy all those metal parts! Tell me, why did you leave all this expensive gear lying about for anyone to pick up? I'm not sure the boys are responsible enough to have access to this kind of kit Mrs Green. The tent in Adam's back garden had more up to the minute gadgets than my team could ever dream of." "I won it all" Davey rushes out his words, "a science competition, design a working space rocket. You remember mum?" Mrs Green nods dubiously at Davey but nobody is buying it. "It's alright Davey, we know your dad gave you all his prototypes when he worked for us and he is probably still doing the same now he works for himself. Tell me though. This creature you've found. Have you discovered what it is yet? How it has come to live in Adam's garden and more importantly where is it now?"

Chapter 20

"That's enough gentlemen the boys have explained, and it is way past their bedtime so if you don't mind…" Mrs Green practically shoved the men out of the house. Davey and I turned to go back through the back door to the tree house. "And just where do you think you two are going? I think you had better come clean and explain exactly what has been going on." I've never seen Mrs Green be quite as stern, she was quite frightening stood there in her enormous fluffy pink dressing gown and slippers.

Davey and I exchange glances, we need to come up with a better story but I'm all out of ideas let alone convincing ones. "Let me in Adam," the voice nudged into my head. "She needs to know the truth." I know that the dinosaur is right so I turn the handle of the kitchen door there stands the Lesothosaurus no taller than an Alsatian dog but unmistakably a dinosaur, not an animatronics puppet. A living, breathing piece of pre-history. He walks forwards on two legs into the brightly lit kitchen. WHAM! Mrs Green slams into the floor unable to comprehend the impossible.

Mrs Green is out cold on the kitchen floor! I feel as though I'm in some kind of Hollywood film set, surely this cannot be happening. Finally Davey manages to bring his mum round but all she does is stare unblinking at the archaic looking creature standing in the doorway of her kitchen. Then she does the most amazing thing. She gets up off the floor and totally ignores the fact that there is the first living dinosaur for over 64 million years standing there watching her in her kitchen, and she makes a cup of tea!!!! A cup of tea!!!! We are facing the problem of what to do with our amazing discovery and all she can do is make a cup of tea. I honestly don't think I will ever understand adults. "Um, Mrs Green?" I ask tentatively, "are you ok? I mean it is a bit of a shock seeing 'Sothy'" Davey looks at me and mouths the name back at me. "Well we have to call him something and I thought Sothy was kind of soft and nice, and a lot shorter than 'the Lesothosaurus', not to mention much easier to say! So anyway Mrs Green I know it has been a shock but we really need your help. I'm sure those men will come back they have Davey's data and everything. What if they want to take Sothy away? That wouldn't be fair. All he wants to do is live quietly at the bottom of our garden munching my dad's compost and I will make sure he gets enough water from now on so no-one needs to even know he exists." Mrs Green holds up her hand to stop me going any further. "Adam! A shock! I'm not even sure there is anything stood in my kitchen right now I am sure I am having some kind of breakdown and as for how you think you know what it wants are you trying to tell me you are communicating with this thing by telepathy? See I am actually going mad! Cuckoo! Crazy! I must see Dr Watts in the morning!" Obviously able to follow the flow of the conversation Sothy slowly moves towards Mrs Green and nudges her hand with his head. She then lets out the most amazingly piercing scream I have ever heard. Suddenly it is pitch black. The back door caves in and people are shouting to get down and move away from the beast. I am pushed to the ground trying to get to Sothy as he squeals. He is trying to get past the men blocking the only way outside into the back garden he knows he has nowhere to go but has to try he rushes forwards managing to knock one of the men off his feet but is caught by a huge net draped over the doorway. The last thing I hear in my head are his hysterical pleas of help as he is bundle into a crate and secured in the back of a van. I try to run out of the door to follow but I am stopped by the two men who have now composed themselves and stand guard at Davey's now wrecked kitchen door.

Chapter 21

Davey and I are taken to the local hospital to make sure we are not hurt. I keep explaining that we are fine. That Sothy only wanted to be left alone and that now those men have him it is Sothy they should be worried about. Instead they tell me to calm down or they will have to give me a sedative as I am disturbing the other patients. Davey is silent. Being the perfect patient I scream at him. How can he just sit there and let them take Sothy away and probably hurt him? Then I'm asleep.

I wake up feeling groggy with mum and dad sitting next to my bed. They look strange sat their in sequins and brightly coloured lycra against the insipid bluey green curtains of our local hospital. Their faces look like clowns with their stage make up garish in the hospital strip lighting. They brighten a bit as I mutter "I want to go home".

After a lot of concerned looks from the nurses and doctors I am allowed home. They want me to stay and see a psychiatrist. I'm not sure what they have been told but I'm pretty sure it's not the truth.

Who would believe it anyway if they hadn't seen it with their own eyes? There is no way I'm staying here talking about my feelings when all I want to do is find Sothy. I need to make sure he is ok. So for now I need to play at being the good little boy who saw nothing and is not going to get upset about an imaginary creature he conjures up from his head... hey of course now I get it! Davey is so clever. I never should have doubted him! He was playing the game from the moment we got in here, so he could get home. I should have known he wouldn't let me or Sothy down. He will have a plan I'm sure of it. The first thing I will do when I convince them all that I'm fine is talk to Davey, he is great at planning and he must know where those guys work. Maybe we can even get his dad to help... if we can make him believe us that is...

To be continued

20724222R00039

Printed in Great Britain
by Amazon